Walt Disney's

GOOFY-
ON-THE-HILLSIDE

GROLIER
BOOK CLUB EDITION

First American Edition. Copyright © 1982 by The Walt Disney Company. All rights reserved under International and Pan-American Copyright Conventions. Published in the United States by Random House, Inc., New York, and simultaneously in Canada by Random House of Canada Limited, Toronto. Originally published in Denmark as EN GOD VEN ER GULD VAERD by Gutenberghus Gruppen, Copenhagen. Copyright © 1981 by Walt Disney Productions. ISBN: 0-394-85112-9

6 7 8 9   F G H I J K

There was once a simple fellow named Goofy
who lived on the side of a hill.

He was called Goofy-on-the-Hillside.

His only neighbor was a kind farmer
named Mrs. Hay.

Goofy and Mrs. Hay
were good friends.

They never quarreled.

If Goofy's apple tree
dropped apples into
Mrs. Hay's yard, did
Mrs. Hay mind?

Not at all!

If Mrs. Hay's cow ate Goofy's grass, did Goofy mind?

Never!

"A good friend is worth more than a bag of gold," Mrs. Hay always said.

Now Mrs. Hay needed some money to fix up her farm.

"Goofy," she said, "will you take my cow to town and sell it?"

"Of course," said Goofy.

Goofy tied a rope to the cow
and set off for town.

Soon Goofy saw a man
who was riding a horse.
"If only I had a horse!"
said Goofy. "Then I could
ride instead of walk."

The man heard what Goofy said.

"Say, I could use a cow," said the man.

"Do you want to trade your cow for my horse?"

"It's a deal!" said Goofy.

So Goofy and the man made a trade.

Goofy climbed onto the horse's back.
"GIDDY-UP!" he said.

The horse took off so fast that
Goofy almost lost his hat.

The horse went faster and faster.
"WHOA!" cried Goofy. "WHOA!"

The horse stopped so quickly that
Goofy flew right off its back.

Along came a woman pushing a pig
in a wheelbarrow.

"Look at that!" said Goofy. "If only
I had a pig instead of a horse!"

The woman heard what Goofy said.

"Young man," said the woman. "Give me that horse and you can have this pig."

"It's a deal!" said Goofy.

So the woman gave her pig to Goofy.

Then the woman rode off with her wheelbarrow.

"Come on, pig!" said Goofy.

But the pig did not move.

Goofy gave the pig a push.
The pig still did not move.

Goofy pushed harder and harder.

That pig would not budge.

Goofy lay down to rest.

Along came a boy with a goat.

The goat was skipping and prancing—
just as merrily as could be.

"Aw, shucks!" said Goofy. "If only
I had a goat instead of a pig!"

The boy heard what Goofy said.

"Hey, mister!" said the boy.
"Would you like to trade your pig
for my goat?"

"It's a deal!" said Goofy.

The boy dropped corn in front of the pig.
The pig followed the boy down the road.

The goat followed Goofy.

HIPPITY-SKIPPITY!

That goat knew how to walk!

By and by Goofy was thirsty.
He bent down to get a drink of water.

That goat knew how to butt, too!
He butted Goofy right into the water.

Goofy sat up and
looked at the goat.
Now the goat was
eating his hat!

Along came a girl
with a hen.
 The hen was
fast asleep.

"Oh, my!" said Goofy. "If only
I had a hen instead of a goat!"

The girl heard what Goofy said.

"Excuse me," said the girl. "Would you trade that goat for this hen?"

"You bet!" said Goofy.

So the girl took the goat for the hen.

Goofy was going along happily
when the hen woke up.
Was she surprised to see Goofy!
FLIP-FLAP-FLUTTER!
She flew out of his arms...

...and landed on the branch
of a tree.

Goofy climbed up to get the hen.
CRACK! went a branch.
Up flew the hen!
Down tumbled Goofy!

Along came
an old woman
with a basket
of eggs.

"Eggs!" cried Goofy. "That's what I need!"

"Would you like to trade your hen for these eggs?" asked the old woman.

"Yes, indeed!" said Goofy.

So the old woman took the eggs out of the basket and put them in Goofy's hat.

Goofy set off with the eggs.
But he tripped on a root in the road.
Down went Goofy!
SPLAT! went the eggs.

Only two eggs were not broken.

"Still, two eggs are better than none,"
said Goofy.

At last Goofy reached town.
By this time he was very hungry.
"I must eat something before I sell
these eggs for Mrs. Hay," he said.

Goofy went into a bakery.
"I want to get some bread," he said.

"Ten cents a loaf," said the baker.
"All I have are these eggs," said Goofy.

"Give me the eggs and I will give you
a loaf of bread," said the baker.

"It's a deal!" said Goofy.

So Goofy made his last trade.

It turned out to be his best.

"What a day!" said Goofy. "My neighbor wanted me to sell her cow, so I traded it—"

"You traded a cow for two eggs?" cried the baker.

"Of course not!" said Goofy. "I traded
the cow for a horse, the horse for a pig,
the pig for a goat, the goat for a hen, and
the hen for some eggs, but most of them broke."

"Your neighbor is going to be
very angry," said the baker.
"Not at all," said Goofy.
"We are good friends."

"I would like to see a friend
as good as that!" said the baker.

"Then come with me," said Goofy.
So the baker closed his shop and
went home with Goofy.

Mrs. Hay was glad to see Goofy and his new friend, the baker.

"Did you sell my cow?" she asked.

"Not exactly," said Goofy. "I traded it for a...for a loaf of bread."

"A loaf of bread!" cried Mrs. Hay.

"Yes," said Goofy. "I was hungry."

"Well, if you were hungry I'm glad you could eat," said Mrs. Hay.

"But now I cannot fix up my farm,"
said Mrs. Hay. "I have no money."

"I can fix up your farm," said Goofy.

"And I can help," said the baker.

They built a new stone wall.

They repaired the barn roof.

And they painted the barn.

Then the baker made a chocolate cake.

"Thanks for your help," said Mrs. Hay.

"That is what friends are for," said
the baker.

"And you know," said Goofy, "a good
friend is worth more than a bag of gold."

And he was right!